Even though the town had grown large, the old owl still sat in the Town Hall tower, reminiscing about his youth when his friends roamed the meadows and he was able to scare them with his swoops.

"In those days we played wonderful games!" the owl sighed. "You spread your wings and life was one big celebration. Hoo! Hoo! Is there anybody left down there?"

At that very moment, a small bird thudded against the owl's side and sang out, distraught: "Help me please, kind and wise owl. Show me the way to Africa, I have to get back there immediately."

"Am I kind, am I wise?" the owl savored the dove's words.

"Well, you're kind if you are helpful," said the dove. "And you are wise if you understand when there is trouble. A sand storm flung me here and now I want to go back home."

"How can I help you when all I can see properly are my memories?" the owl asked. "My wings have grown heavy, I haven't even got the strength to move them."

"You're covered with sand," the dove observed. "Let me clean you up."

"Thank you," said the owl. "You help me and then I'll help you. It's as simple as that."

"That's right," said the dove. "We're wise and simple."

The dove spent all night cleaning up the owl. At dawn, the owl scrabbled to his feet and sighed happily. "I had a wonderful dream. An angel was floating over my head telling me a beautiful fairy tale."

"That was me," the dove cooed cheerfully. "Now try your wings."

The owl spread his wings and flapped them.

"Thank you, little one, for cleaning my feathers," the owl exclaimed. "I feel as *light* as a feather. Now we're ready to start looking for your home."

The owl and the dove flew over the city roofs, over villages, valleys and mountains. But when a vast ocean appeared below them, the old owl started feeling tired.

"Your home is too far. We've got to have a rest," said the owl anxiously.

The dove felt scared. The open sea spread out under them. Not a single ship was visible.

"You'll just have to keep going," the dove encouraged her friend.

"I can't," said the owl and spread his wings, preparing for his last flight.

Then the dove remembered a song she had learned from her sister and sang with all her heart:

If you're in need of help, you can always ask,
your wings get light if you're helped with a task
the strong are able to carry weak ones ashore,
the strong give the weak the power to do more
when the wind is behind them.

In no time at all, a bubbling noise emanated from the sea. Out of nowhere, a large dark island appeared below the owl and the dove and the birds made a speedy landing on it. After a while, the island rose higher, opened its large mouth and said: "I heard your song in the depths of the ocean and came to the surface right away."

The owl and the dove realized that the island was actually a whale!

"You saved us," said the owl gratefully. "I'd already imagined myself down there among the fish. We're heading to Africa."

"That's where I'm heading, too, to go to the rescue of my brothers and sisters."

"What's the matter with them?" asked the owl.

"I don't know yet, they've got something to say to humans," said the whale. "Maybe there's a human who's in need of help."

When the dove, the owl and the whale arrived at the coast of Africa the following morning, they were met with a strange sight. The whale's four siblings were lying on the beach, exhausted and thirsty.

"Get away from there right now!" the whale shouted. "You can live only in water! "

"We can't move," the youngest sibling squealed. "We wanted to say to the humans that the sea belongs to us, too. We also exist!"

"The strong give the weak the power to do more when the wind is behind them!" sang the dove.

"We've got to act fast," said the owl to the whale. "Squirt some water, swing your tail!"

The whale did not waste any time. Quickly he raised great waves around his siblings with his tail. For the whole day he splashed water onto the beach. By the evening the whales were finally surrounded by water and swam back into the sea.

"Never, ever go on land again," said the whale. "We'll have to find other ways to make the humans understand."

"Absolutely right," said the owl. "Stay where you are in the water: you'll be needed someday."

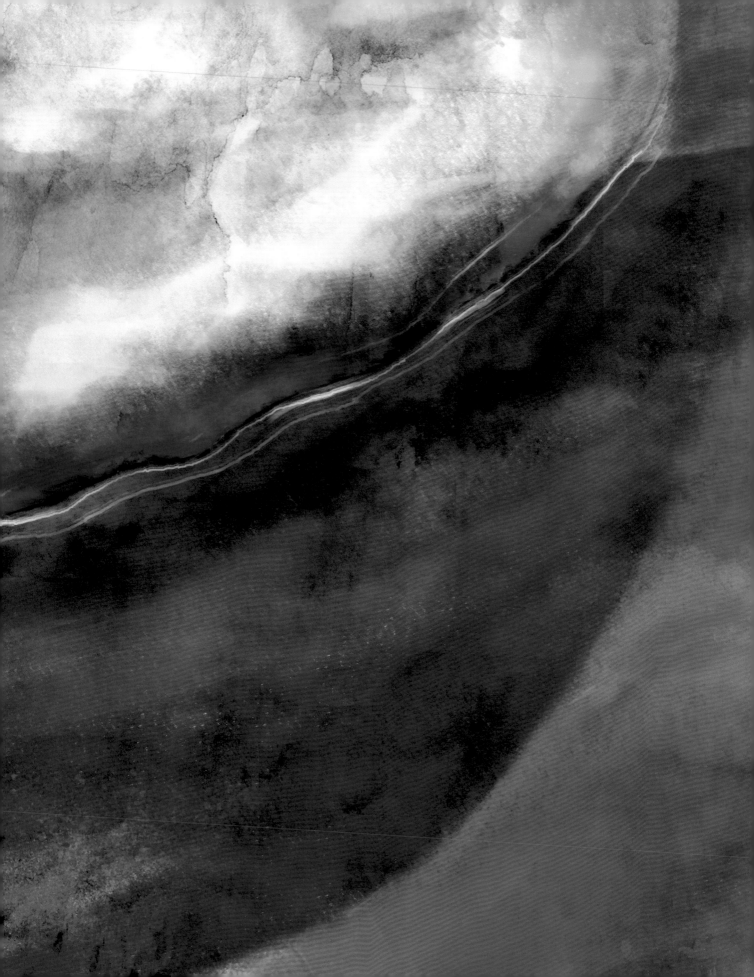

The owl and the dove flew inland through the sandstorm to where the dove's home tree once stood. But the site had become one big desert.

"This used to be a dense forest," the dove sighed sadly. She then flew into the sky and burst into song: "I'm a small bird and I want to enjoy some peace and quiet!"

The dove's words made the owl smile.

"Where there's a will, there's a way," the owl said. "I want the same thing."

It became calm, there was a moment's peace, then a little gust of wind arrived and said: "It's not my fault that the sand comes along with me. I do all sorts of good things, too: I'm refreshing when it's hot and I provide wind for ships' sails. I'm no ill wind."

"But deserts! Remember the deserts!" the owl said with a cough.

"I do remember," the wind said. "But what can we do?"

The dove had an idea. "We've got to plant some trees. But where can we get some seeds? There's not a pine cone in sight around here."

"I'm about to embark on a round-the-world trip, I can take a message," said the wind. "I'll be a real whirlwind!"

The wind clasped the owl and the dove's wishes to his large bosom, twisted and turned merrily, and set off. At the speed of a hurricane he carried the message across mountains and oceans to many continents.

Everywhere the wind went, he took along a breeze of good will. In the Americas, the wind whispered the message into a mountain lion's ear; in China, he gave it to a panda; in Australia, to a koala; and in Africa, to a gorilla.

The strong give the weak the power to do more
when the wind is behind them.

And the animals were so cheered by the message that they all decided to leave immediately.

"I'll take along an elm seed," the mountain lion mused.

"I'll go bearing a eucalyptus seed," the koala thought.

"I'll take an obeche seed. There's no better gift than an obeche," the the gorilla reflected.

"I'll take a spruce seed," the panda decided. "The spruce is everyone's festive tree."

The koala decided to cross the sea on a raft. He lay on top of the wooden blocks, paddling with his paws, but he was not strong enough to fight the big waves. Hanging his head, the koala cub returned to his island.

The mountain lion, brave as she was, also tried and plunged into the water, but after swimming a yard realized that there was no way she would make it all the way to Africa.

The panda set out on foot but was able to trudge only as far as the beach before his thick fur was already steaming in the heat. The sad panda stared at the sun setting beyond the sea.

The gorilla decided to hitch-hike. He kept his thumb out for five days but nobody offered him a lift.

A month went by and then another. The owl and the dove got worried.

"Nobody's coming," said the owl.

"Nobody's heard our plea," the dove added fretfully.

"I passed on your plea to everyone," said the wind. "But the journey is long, and I can't fly them here."

Then the mighty song of the whales boomed from the sea.

"The strong give the weak the power to do more when the wind is behind them," the whales sang in unison.

"We'll go and bring your friends here," said the biggest whale.

"A whale is the best ship," lisped the smallest one.

Five black backs were soon speeding across the waves far beyond the horizon and it took only a week for the entourage to return. The panda, the mountain lion, the koala and the gorilla stood like magnificent sails on the backs of the whales and, on reaching the African shore, they started wandering over the mountains to the desert. The tired but happy whales stayed behind to have a rest in the morning mist after their mission.

On reaching their destination, the animals started
to work immediately. Together they dug a big hole and
planted the seeds in it. Then they all sang together a song
taught to them by the dove and waited for a tree to grow.

We have one common wish
for the shelter of great forests
as Nature's warm embrace
is the well of our common bliss

Now it was the sun's turn to get worried. She heard the
friends' song and said: "I give out warmth but no tree can
grow without water."
"I wonder where we can get water?" the dove asked
mournfully. "It never rains here. Should we cry to water
the tree? Our tears won't be enough for that!"

All the same, the animals cried until nightfall, until they finally fell asleep totally exhausted. In the morning they were woken up by the sun's first rays. Suddenly the animals huddled together, frightened: a small biped was approaching them across the desert.

The child reached the animals, smiled and said: "I heard you crying and came to help you. Who's thirsty?"

They all nodded and the child fished out a clay pot from his backpack.

"We've had a well in our village for a long time; that's where the water comes from," he explained. "Help yourselves."

The animals drank some water and perked up. In turn, each was also allowed to pour some water on the seeds.

The koala became poetic. "Here's a drop of water for the great and small, for new lives for all! We protect the water."

"We protect the air," said the panda.

"We protect the plants," the mountain lion added.

"We protect the animals," the gorilla whispered.

"We protect the sea," the whales sang from faraway in the sea.

"These are drops of life for the humans, too," said the child.

Just then, a little seedling lifted its head from the sand, looked at everyone and said brightly: "Morning."

"Many happy returns, little one," the dove and the owl sang joyously. "It's your birthday today!"

Drops of Life is also a well-known children's play and has been performed in over eighty countries. The play, also written by Esko-Pekka Tiitinen, supports the environmental campaign of ENO's (Environment Online) netschool. Through the campaign, school children have planted millions of trees all over the world.

Environment Online (ENO) is a global virtual school and network for sustainable development. Schools around the world study the same environmental topics and share their learning results with their local communities and worldwide on the web. The themes cover forests, water, biodiversity, climate change, ecological footprints, cultural issues and more. Material and structured courses for each theme are available in English on the ENO website. The students' ages range from 10 to 18 years.

Tree planting has been one of ENO's most popular activities since 2004. Since the beginning, about 10,000 schools in 152 countries have planted trees. This long-term tree-planting campaign will wrap-up in 2017 when Finland celebrates its 100th anniversary. The ENO schools' target is to plant 100 million trees, six million of which were planted as of May 2011.

Climate change has been a regular theme in the ENO Programme since 2002 and has been studied through different projects. Students have written articles about the impact of climate change, hosted radio interviews, performed plays that are available on the Internet, and marched during ENO campaign weeks.

ENO was founded in 2000 and is coordinated by the ENO Programme Association based in Joensuu, Finland. ENO has numerous partner organizations and networks including the United Nations Environment Programme and the University of Eastern Finland. It has won 15 national and international awards and recognitions:

*   European Umbrella Project for NetDays, 2000, European Commission, Paris, France
*   Third Prize in EcoG@llery Europe, 2000, Barcelona, Spain
*   Third Prize in Childnet Awards, 2001, Washington DC, USA
*   Finalist in the Stockholm Challenge Awards, 2002 and 2004, Stockholm, Sweden
*   Finalist in the Global Junior Challenge Awards, 2002 and 2004, Rome, Italy
*   Cyber Oscar Award, UN Summit on Information Society, 2003, Geneve, Switzerland
*   WWF Panda Prize, 2004, Finland
*   Finalist with a special mention in the Stockholm Challenge Awards, 2006, Stockholm, Sweden
*   Winner in the Global Junior Challenge Awards, 2007, Rome, Italy
*   Finalist in the Stockholm Challenge Awards, 2008, Stockholm, Sweden
*   Energy Globe Awards, 2009, Prague, Czech Republic
*   Forestry Achievement of the Year, 2009, Helsinki, Finland
*   Official status in the Ministry of Education, 2010, Israel

ENO Programme website: www.enoprogramme.org
ENO Tree Planting Day: www.enotreeday.net